Change Sings

A
Children's
Anthem

Amanda Gorman   Loren Long

VIKING

I can hear change humming
In its loudest, proudest song.

I don't fear change coming,
And so I sing along.

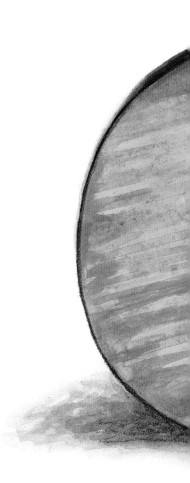

I scream with the skies
Of red and blue streamers.

I dream with the cries
Of tried-and-true dreamers.

I'm a chant that rises and rings.

There is hope where my change sings.

Though some don't understand it,
Those windmills of mysteries,

I sing with all the planet,
And its hills of histories.

I hum with a hundred hearts,
Each of us lifting a hand.

I use my strengths and my smarts,
Take a knee to make a stand.

I'm bright as the light each day brings.

There is love where my change sings.

I show others tolerance,
Though it might take some courage.

I don't make a taller fence,

But fight to build a better bridge.

I talk not only of distances,

From where and how we came.

I also walk our differences,
To show we are the same.

I'm a movement that roars and springs,
There's a wave where my change sings.

Change sings where? There! Inside me.

Because I'm the change I want to see.

As I grow, it grows like seeds.

I am just what the world needs.

I'm the voice where freedom rings.
You're the love your bright heart brings.

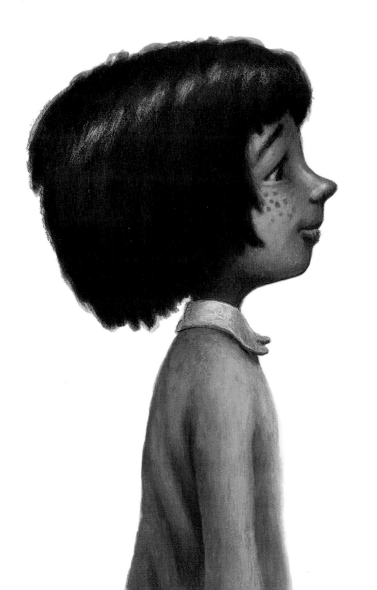

We are the wave starting to spring,
For we are the change we sing.

We're what the world is becoming,
And we know it won't be long.

We all hear change strumming.
Won't you sing along?

For my mom,
who always believed in my voice.
—AG

For Tracy,
who is always a vital part of my work.
—LL

VIKING

An imprint of Penguin Random House LLC, New York

First published in the United States of America by Viking, an imprint of Penguin Random House LLC, 2021

Visit us online at penguinrandomhouse.com.

LIBRARY OF CONGRESS CATALOGING-IN-PUBLICATION DATA IS AVAILABLE.

Manufactured in China

ISBN 9780593203224

1   3   5   7   9   10   8   6   4   2

HH

Design by Jim Hoover   Text set in Moranga and Quacker

The art for this book was created by hand on illustration board, using acrylics and colored pencil.